INSPIRING TRUE STORIES BOOK FOR 6 YEAR OLD BOYS

I AM 6
AND
AMAZING

Inspirational tales About Courage, Self-Confidence and Friendship

Paula Collins

Contents

Introduction

Hello, brave and amazing explorer! Did you know just how special you are? There's no one else in this big, wide world who's quite like you. And that's pretty fantastic! Among billions of people, you shine in your very own way. You're smart, funny, strong, and absolutely one-of-a-kind. Always remember that.

Life is full of big and little challenges. Some might seem scary, and others might make you question yourself. But guess what? Everyone feels this way sometimes — your mom, dad, siblings, grandparents, friends, and even people you've never met!

Facing something new or tricky might feel a bit scary, but those moments can end up being the ones you learn from the most. It's okay to make mistakes; just try to find the good in every situation, even the tough ones.

Inside this book, you'll read about kids just like you. They're brave and they face challenges head-on. Sometimes things don't go their way, but they keep trying and learn from everything that happens. When things get tough, they find a special spark inside that keeps them going.

Each story here will show you how these kids find confidence, hope, and bravery in every situation, helping them chase their dreams.

Now it's your turn to shine bright and light up the world around you. Spread your sparkle, face your fears, and soak up life's lessons. Always believe in yourself because you can do anything.

Remember, you are a truly amazing and unique kiddo!"

A New Friend

A Fresh Start

Hi, I'm Liam, I'm 6 years old and I live in a home filled with love with my parents, and my older sister Lisa. Today at school, I saw a girl I didn't know! I found out her name is Sarah. Everyone was looking at her and not saying very nice things about her. They said she was weird, and I just thought, "Why?" Sarah looked quiet, but she wasn't talking to anyone. Her eyes were

staring at the desk as if she had a secret drawing.

I always try to be kind to everyone, like when I share my cookies. But with Sarah, I didn't know what to do. I was a little scared to go and talk to her because others might start saying things about me too. But I also felt sad for her. What if she needs a friend?

After thinking a lot while playing with my crayons, I decided that maybe I should try to be friends with Sarah. But it's hard. It's like when you try to feed a wild animal; you want to help, but you don't know if it will bite you.

My mom always says that being brave is doing things even if they scare you a little. So maybe tomorrow, I can be brave and go talk to Sarah. I don't want her to be alone. I would feel sad

too if nobody wanted to be my friend.

Maybe I can show her my favorite dinosaur book. Everyone likes dinosaurs, right? Or we could draw together. Drawing always makes me happy.

That's what I'll do. I'll be Sarah's friend, even if others don't want to. And who knows, maybe Sarah is super fun!

A Step Forward

Back at school again, and there's Sarah, sitting alone just like yesterday. I started thinking that being alone must not be fun. Sometimes, when I look at Sarah, I feel like I'm watching a

sad movie where you know something the character doesn't. I want to tell her that she can be happy if we talk and play, but it's complicated.

It's strange how something in your heart tells you "Go and talk to her!" but your feet don't

want to move. It's like when you're at the top of a slide and you're scared to slide down, but you know it's going to be fun. That's how I feel about Sarah. I want to go, but something is holding me back.

At recess, I was with my friends talking about school stuff, as usual. But then they started talking bad about Sarah. They said she was weird for always being alone. That made me feel a little sad and angry because Sarah doesn't choose to be alone, I think.

So, without thinking, I said, "Maybe she just needs a friend. What if it's us?" My friends looked at me like I had said I wanted to eat worms. But after a while, one of them said, "Hmm, maybe Liam is right. We could give it a try."

That made me feel a bunch of butterflies in my stomach, but the good kind. Like when you're about to open a present. It was weird but nice to stand up for Sarah. I felt like a superhero in my comics, always saving someone.

New Friends

In the next class, the teacher talked about something called "diversity" and "inclusion". At first, I thought they were names of planets or something science-y. But no, turns out it's about how we're all different but equally important. And that made me think of Sarah.

The teacher said that sometimes, unintentionally, we can make someone feel like they don't belong, just because they're different. That sounded a lot like me. Like when you pick teams to play and someone is always picked last. I wondered if Sarah felt like that, like the last one picked, all the time.

So, at recess, I gathered all my courage, which felt like it was filled with helium, like those balloons that float, and I walked over to Sarah.

I was nervous, my hands were sweating, and I was afraid of saying something silly. But I remembered what the teacher said about being kind and accepting, and that gave me a

little more courage.

I approached and said, "Hi, Sarah. Do you want to play with me?" It was weird because my voice sounded like it wasn't mine, like it was from a cartoon character. But I did it, I talked to her.

At first, Sarah looked surprised, like nobody had talked to her in years. But then she smiled, and that smile was like the sun coming out just for us. We talked a bit, and yes, it was a little awkward, but it was also great. Like discovering a new game or a candy you've never tried.

Tomorrow, I'm going to invite Sarah to play again. And maybe, just maybe, she'll start becoming friends with my other friends too. Because we all deserve to be picked, not just in games, but also in friendship.

Discovering a New World

Wow! Today was amazing because Sarah and I spent a lot of time together. We found out that we both love to draw and that we have the same favorite cartoons. It's like we've been friends forever but didn't know it. It's weird but cool at the same time.

At recess, we drew a big castle with dragons and princesses who know karate. Yes, because who says princesses can't be black belts? Sara made a princess who looks like she could win any battle, and I drew some really cool dragons.

Today I learned that being brave doesn't mean not being afraid. It means doing something despite the fear. And although talking to Sarah was super scary, it was also one of the best things I've ever done. I feel like today I did

something important, not just for Sarah but for me too.

I've learned that each person is like a book with a different story. And if you don't get close to getting to know them, it's like that book stays closed forever. How boring would the world be if we only read the same book over and over again, right?

Two Languages

The Big Mix-Up

Hi! I'm Arjun, and today was another one of those days. I'm 6 years old, almost 7, and I live at home with my Mom and Dad, who come from India.

Speaking English and Hindi should give me superpowers, right? Well, at school, it feels more like having two left feet. Just this morning, I mixed both languages while talking to the teacher. I ended up saying "thank you" and "dhanyavaad" together. She looked at me as if I had spoken Martian. I wanted the ground to swallow me up.

It's weird because switching from one language to another is like breathing at home. But at school, it's like speaking in secret codes that no one else understands.

But not everything is bad. I love my English and Indian culture. It's just that sometimes I wish they fit together a little better, like puzzle pieces that fit smoothly. Anyway, I've seen it as an adventure. After all, who says being a little different is a bad thing?

Backpack Volcano and New Friendship

If you thought yesterday was a show, wait until you hear about today. In the middle of a test, my backpack decided it was a good time to act like a volcano. All my school stuff erupted across the classroom, and to top it off, my Hindi story landed in the middle of the scene. I felt like a giant spotlight exposed all my secrets.

But then something unexpected happened. Oliver came to my rescue! Before this, Oliver was just another boy in my class, not really my friend yet. But his curiosity was sparked when he saw what happened with me. "Do you speak two languages?" he asked with genuine amazement. I explained about my heritage, and to my surprise, he thought it was awesome. We spent recess together, exchanging words in English and Hindi. Oliver was eager to learn, and I was thrilled to teach.

As we laughed and stumbled over pronunciations, a bond formed between us. For the first time in a long time, I felt like I wasn't the only puzzle piece in the wrong place. It was the beginning of a beautiful friendship, rooted in curiosity and understanding.

So, today, I learned two things: embarrassing moments can be the beginning of something great, and maybe being unique isn't so bad after all.

Connecting Cultures

Today was one of those epic days, ones that make you see the world with different eyes. It turns out that telling Oliver about my life has made the rest of the class interested in my culture and  where I come from. At lunch time, our table

went from being the typical snack table to becoming the language class. There we were, transforming a corner of the dining room into a Hindi class, with everyone trying to say "Namaste" (a respectful greeting), "Alvida" (goodbye), "Dost" (friend), and "Dhanyavaad" (thank you) with more or less success. Between laughter and the occasional pronunciation worthy of a viral video, English and Hindi began to sound like the musical band of our little adventure.

But I didn't stop there, oh no. I told my class about Diwali, is like a super party of bright lights celebrated by some people around the world. Imagine your birthday or Christmas, but with many, many more sparkles and fireworks. People light small lamps called "diyas" and place them around their homes, making everything look magical. They also eat delicious sweets and spend time with their families. It's a way to celebrate goodness, happiness, and the start of new and bright things. It's super special and beautiful! And

don't even let me talk about Sunday Thali meals, which are typical Indian food.

My new friends were very excited, hanging on to every word as if it were the last episode of their favorite series. And the best part is, they started sharing their own stories as if suddenly we all had something to tell. I learned about words I didn't even know existed, foods my taste buds need to try, and traditions that are weirder than a green dog.

It was as if our table had turned into a human Google Maps, but without the part where you get lost along the way. Suddenly, I realized that my quirks, those things I thought made me the odd one out, are actually what brought us together. Diversity isn't that giant wall that separates us; it's more like the suspension bridge we're building word by word, story by story.

Today, I've felt more connected than ever, not just with my friends, but with that big world

out there. And all thanks for sharing a little bit of who I am.

Loving Who I Am

Wow! What days I've had! They've been like an emotional rollercoaster, but the kind that leaves you with a giant smile and wanting to ride it again. At first, I felt like an alien in my school, with my double language and the traditions of two different worlds. Imagine walking with a glowing sign above your head that blinks, saying, "I'm different!" Every time I opened my mouth to speak, it was like that sign shone even brighter.

But something changed. By sharing my story, I've discovered that being different isn't a warning sign but an invitation to an adventure. My friends started asking me questions, not because they wanted to point me out, but because they genuinely wanted to know more about me. They asked me how to say "star" or

"sea" in Hindi, and their eyes lit up with each new answer. Suddenly, I wasn't the extra puzzle piece; I was the piece everyone wanted to see where it fit.

Through this transformation, I came to realize that my quirks, those things that make me me, are actually disguised superpowers. I've realized that loving myself means embracing all those parts, even the ones I once thought were too weird or different.

So, yes, I've learned to love myself just as I am, with all those quirks that make me unique. I'm grateful for each one of them because, without them, I wouldn't be Arjun, the boy from two worlds who has found his place among friends who appreciate differences as much as I do.

With love, a smile that won't fit on my face, and a heart that's about to burst with happiness,

Arjun

Respecting The Rules

The Visit to Uncle Max

Hi, I'm Henry. Some people think I'm an expert at finding trouble, but I prefer to call myself an "enthusiast of unplanned adventures." Well, my latest "adventure" took place at my Uncle Max's house, which could easily win the prize for the most fun and chaotic place on the planet, thanks to his collection of odd rules

and his two pets: Olaf, a dog who could pass for a bear in disguise, and Mr. Whiskerson, a cat who thinks he's royalty.

When I got to Uncle Max's house, he said I must follow the rules "to keep peace in the kingdom." The new rule is that Olaf cannot enter the house because of Mr. Whiskerson, who looks like a little king with whiskers. I just wanted to play with Olaf inside, but Uncle said if Olaf enters, Mr. Whiskerson might turn into a dragon. Imagine that!

So here I am, thinking about how to make Olaf and Mr. Whiskerson get along. I have some ideas, but I think I'll need the superhero cape I made last year. This is going to be the start of a great adventure!
Wish me luck!

Operation Olaf

I decided to become an expert at playing hide-and-

seek and making secret plans, although, to be honest, it didn't turn out as well as I expected. The mission was clear: get Olaf, the biggest and most drooling dog I have ever met, inside the house without Uncle Max noticing. It sounds easy right? Well it wasn't.

First, I had to wait for the perfect moment. Uncle Max was in the garden, talking on the phone. "Now or never!" I thought. I carefully opened the door, looking around like a spy in a movie. Olaf entered with that "I don't know what's happening, but I like it" face. Everything was going well until Mr. Whiskerson, the cat with the demeanor of an emperor, appeared out of nowhere.

Imagine this: Olaf, as big as a small elephant, and Mr. Whiskerson, with a look that could freeze the sun. They looked at each other. They sniffed each other. And then, as if someone had pressed the madness button, the battle of the century began!

They ran around the room, jumping on furniture, knocking over vases (one of them was Uncle Max's favorite, ouch!), and leaving a trail of destruction. I tried to calm them down and show them that we should be friends by wearing my superhero cape and making peace signs, but I think I just made them think I was playing.

After what seemed like hours but were only a few minutes, I managed to separate them using the ancient technique of distraction with food. But the damage was done. The living room looked like a battlefield after an intense day.

Now I'm sitting on the couch, thinking about how I'm going to explain this to Uncle Max. "It was a science experiment gone wrong," or maybe "I was testing a new theory about animal harmony." Sounds believable, right?
I have to find a way to fix this. Or at least, learn to be better at making plans. Wish me luck!

The Great Cleaning Adventure

If I thought this mischief was an adventure, I had no idea what awaited me. When Uncle Max saw the disaster, his face went through all the colors of the rainbow. At first, I thought he was going to explode like a volcano, but instead, he calmly (well, almost calmly) told me I had to clean it all up.

So, armed with a broom, a rag, and a lot of goodwill, I began my "cleaning adventure." Every piece of trash, every stain on the carpet, reminded me of my little rebellion. "This is going to be easy," I had thought. How wrong I was!

Cleaning the broken vase was like a puzzle without all the pieces. And getting Olaf's hair

off the sofa... well, I think there are still some left as a souvenir. And then there was the matter of Mr. Whiskerson's whiskers, which I found in the strangest places.

In the middle of the cleaning, Uncle Max came to see how it was going. I thought he would get even angrier seeing the slow progress, but instead, he helped me. Together, we did more in an hour than I had done in three. He taught me how to clean better (apparently, there's an art to it too) and, although he didn't say it, I think he was a bit impressed by my determination.

Today I learned two important lessons. The first is that what we do can make others feel bad, and learning from that helps us grow. The second, and perhaps most surprising, is that even in the most difficult situations, you can find learning moments. Uncle Max and I had never spent so much time together, working as a team. It was so special.

So, although it started as the worst day, it didn't end so badly. I have the feeling that, after this experience, things are going to be a bit different between Uncle Max and me.

Lessons and Promises

Today, I woke up in my house thinking about everything that has happened. I've been reflecting a lot on the rules, why they exist, and how my actions can affect others. I realized that, although sometimes rules seem annoying, they're there for a reason. And that reason, more often than I thought, is to keep us safe, both us and those around us.

I've learned that asking for permission before doing something, especially something big or that could be problematic, is a way to show

respect for someone else's decisions and space. Uncle Max had reasons for his rules, and now I see that, if I had followed them, I would have saved myself a lot of trouble (and extra work!) and saved the poor Uncle Max's favorite vase.

So, here I am, promising myself that next time I will think before I act. I don't mean that I will always follow all the rules without asking why. After all, that's part of growing up. But I'm definitely going to be more thoughtful about the rules I choose to break.

Until the next adventure.

Life in The Garden

Surprise in the Garden

Hi there! My name is Noah, and I'm just two days away from turning 6 years old. I live in a house with a big back yard, but what I really love is going to the park nearby. There, they have slides, swings, and many other fun things. I could spend hours and hours there, enjoying it without stopping. However, we

can't always stay for as long as I'd like since Mom has other tasks to attend to. My older brother, David, sometimes joins us, and together we make the day even more fun.

My birthday is coming up soon, and my parents gave me the best early birthday present ever: they turned our back yard into a playground! Imagine, now I have my own secret place with swings, a giant slide, and much more.

Today, as I was exploring my new kingdom, I stumbled upon something unexpected. It wasn't a hidden treasure or a forgotten toy, but a nest of bunnies. They looked as surprised to see me as I was to see them, with their curious little eyes staring at me intently.

I wondered, "Are these bunnies part of the gift?" But soon I realized that this was their home before my park appeared. I felt like I had invaded their space, sort of like when David enters my room without knocking.

Then I remembered something that happened to me once at my grandma's farm. There was a hen, let's call her "Ms. Pecks," who chased me all around the yard just because I got too close to her chicks. It scared me so much that I even fell into a mud puddle. And let me tell you, those hens can run fast!

That got me thinking... I was intruding on the bunnies' territory just like I intruded on Ms. Pecks' and her chicks' area. And I don't want the mommy bunny to think I'm some sort of dangerous giant coming to bother them. I

want to be, how should I put it? A good neighbor, I guess.

So I decided I should act with respect. Today, instead of playing in my super park, I sat on the side and drew. Yes, I drew portraits, well sort of, of "Hopper", "Floppy", and "Fluffy" (that's what I named the three bunnies). Drawing rabbits is harder than it looks, especially when they move so much. Every time I tried to draw Fluffy, it ended up looking like cotton candy with eyes.

So, for now, I left them their territory. It was a bit tough, especially with my new slide waiting. But I understand that sharing is more than just handing out things; it's also about giving others their room.

Tomorrow is my birthday party, and I've become a mini researcher. I was determined to learn all about the bunnies to make sure they could feel safe and happy while we play. After all, sharing is caring, right?

The Most Special Birthday in the Garden

Finally, the big day arrived, along with a party none of us would ever forget. My friends were super excited to enjoy the new park in my back yard, and I was just as thrilled to show them how we would share this space with the bunnies respectfully.

Before we started playing, I gathered everyone and talked to them about our furry neighbors. I showed them the "safe zone" we had prepared especially for the bunnies, marked clearly with small fences so everyone knew that area was just for them.

We also set up alternate play times: we would enjoy an hour of games and then take a 15-minute break. During these breaks, we had the chance to observe the bunnies from afar,

learning more about nature and the importance of sharing our space kindly.

The party turned into a festival for all the garden inhabitants, including the bunnies "Hopper", "Floppy", and "Fluffy". We decorated with everyone in mind, with cheerful colors that wouldn't scare the animals, and we prepared snacks for both my human friends and our rabbit friends. Together, we filled the day with laughter, games, and moments of learning about living in harmony.

The Adventure of Sharing

From this adventure, I learned that sharing goes beyond giving material things; it's about sharing moments, experiences, and, above all, our surroundings considerately. Sometimes,

the best friends are those you'd never expect to have.

In the end, my birthday wasn't just a celebration of another year of life, but also the beginning of a new way of seeing my world. My back yard transformed from a simple green area into a gathering place for friends of all species.

I learned that sharing is much more than handing out toys or snacks; it's about sharing our world, respecting all living beings that inhabit it. And with a little creativity and a lot of respect, there's always enough space for everyone.

Until the next adventure!

Noah, the little back yard explorer.

The New Hamster

My New Friend, Maurice

Hello! I'm William, and today is the coolest day ever! I'm 6 years old and I live in this really quiet neighborhood with my Mom, my Dad, and my little brother, who is a huge fan of cartoons. Every day feels like an adventure waiting to happen. And guess what? I absolutely adore animals.

After like a thousand years (well, maybe just a couple of months) of begging Mom and Dad, they finally said yes! I'm going to have a hamster! I'm going to call him Maurice, because it sounds like a super elegant and adventurous hamster name.

At first, I wasn't sure I wanted a hamster. I wanted a dinosaur, but it turns out they've been extinct for a long time. So, a hamster was option B. But when I saw Maurice in the store, it was love at first sight. He's like a little ball of fur that knows how to look straight into your soul. And those bright eyes, it's as if he understands every word I say!

Mom says it's a big responsibility and that I have to feed him, clean his cage, and make sure he exercises. I told her no problem, because I already take care of my little brother (which is almost the same, but louder).

So here I am, ready to be the best hamster owner in the world. Maurice is not only going to be my pet; he's going to be my friend in all the adventures we're sure to have. I can't wait to see what the future holds!

It's going to be an incredible journey!

Adventures and Misadventures with Maurice

Today I discovered that having a hamster is like having a superhero baby: small but with great powers. Especially, the power to keep you super busy.

First, I decided that Maurice needed a palace, not just a cage. So, I built a mega cardboard tunnel with towers, bridges, and even a maze. I think Maurice feels like the king of his little kingdom. I see him

running back and forth, exploring every corner. He's the bravest explorer in the world!

But it wasn't all fun. Mom reminded me (for the millionth time) that I had to clean Maurice's cage. I thought it would be easy, but did you know that hamsters are real artists of mess? The more I cleaned, the more mess I found. It was as if Maurice had a secret party while I was away.

And just when I thought I had finished, Maurice decided to make a dramatic escape. He ran so fast that he almost became a flying hamster. I had to go on a rescue mission in my own room. Finally, I found him hidden behind some books. I think he just wanted to prove that he's a master of hide-and-seek.

So, I've learned that being responsible means more than just giving Maurice food and water. It means building castles, being a mess detective, and going on rescue missions. And to think that all this is just the beginning!

The Great Mystery of Maurice

Today was the longest day of my life. I came home, excited to tell Maurice about my day at school, only to discover that Maurice had disappeared! The door of his cage was open, and no matter  how much I searched, there was no sign of him anywhere.

First, I thought it was one of his tricks, like the great Houdini, but then I started to worry. What if he had gone on an adventure on his own and couldn't come back? Or worse, what if he met the monster under my bed?

I searched every corner of the house, calling him and promising him a feast of sunflower seeds if he returned. Nothing. My parents

joined the search, and even my little brother paused his favorite TV program to help, which is a miracle.

I felt really sad and guilty. How could I have left the door open? I promised to take care of Maurice, and now, I didn't know if he was scared and alone in some dark corner.

But just when we were about to give up, I heard a noise behind the washing machine. And there he was, Maurice, looking at me as if nothing had happened. The relief I felt was immense! I hugged him (carefully) and promised to be the best hamster guardian in the world. Maurice is back, safe and sound. It was like finding a hidden treasure, except the treasure was my little furry friend. The happiness I felt seeing him well is indescribable.

Today I learned that being responsible is super important, especially when someone depends on you. And Maurice, well, I think he

learned that there's no place like his warm and safe home (or maybe he just wanted more sunflower seeds), and I'm determined to be even better for Maurice.

Learning About Responsibility

After finding Maurice safe and sound, I've deeply reflected on what it really means to have a pet. This experience has opened my eyes to the importance of responsibility. I realized that taking care of Maurice is not just about enjoying his company, but ensuring his well-being, safety, and happiness. This incident taught me that being responsible means always paying attention, making decisions with others' happiness in mind, and learning from our mistakes to avoid repeating them.

I promise to be more attentive to my little friend's needs. I now understand that responsibility is a daily commitment that goes beyond words; it's demonstrated through

daily actions that ensure the care and protection of those who depend on us.

As we look to the future, I'm excited for all the adventures Maurice and I will share, knowing each day is an opportunity to be a better caregiver and friend to him. Responsibility is a journey, not a destination, and I'm ready to continue learning and growing alongside Maurice.

Weekend at the Beach

¡What a Heatwave!

Hi, I'm Mason, I'm 6 years old, and I live in a house on the outskirts of the city with my parents. Let me tell you, today when I woke up, the first thing I felt was like the sun and I were playing hide and seek, and it found me under the sheets. Phew! Can someone explain to me why it has to be SO hot? If it were up to

me, I'd live in an igloo with penguins as neighbors.

Let's see... Today is Friday and the long weekend begins. That means no school for three whole days! That should make me happy, but there's a small problem: the heat and I are not friends. Can you imagine melting like a strawberry ice cream? Well, that's how I feel.

Mom says summer is for enjoying, for going out and jumping under the sun. I say it's for staying indoors, with the air conditioning on full blast. And I have the perfect plan: convince Mom to go to the mall. That's my salvation, the cool and icy air that I love so much.

So, while I plan how to convince her, I'm going to practice my "I'm suffering unbearable heat"

face. Although I don't think I need much practice... It's just so hot!

I'll tell you how my master plan goes later. Cross your fingers for me!

With lots of heat and a bit of hope,

Mason

Beach Surprise!

You won't believe this! Today, just as I was about to show Mom my "I'm suffering unbearable heat" face, she surprised me: we're going to the beach! Can someone tell her that the beach is basically the sun in its biggest and sandiest form?

And as if the sun and the sand weren't enough company, guess who else is coming: Aunt Emma and my cousin Lisa. Auntie is cool, but Lisa... let's just say she's as "energetic" as a tornado in a toy store.

Well, when we got there, Lisa dragged me to build a sandcastle. I swear, doing that is like trying to stick bricks together with gum. And just as I was putting the flag on the tallest tower, BAM! Lisa throws sand in my face. In  my face! If I wanted a natural mask, I would have asked for one.

Aunt Emma became my hero. She rushed me to the nearest faucet and washed my face like she was panning for gold in a river. And then, with the patience of a saint, she put drops in my eye that stung more than a mosquito bite.

Between us, I felt like turning the castle into a sand trap for Lisa. But I didn't. My face and pride hurt, but Mom always says that "revenge is never good." Although, I admit that at that moment, I didn't quite agree with Mom.

Now I'm here, getting the last grain of sand out of my eye. Mom says sand is magical and holds memories. I just hope it doesn't hold the memory of my "Lisa, I'm going to..." face. Well, you know.

At the end of the day, Aunt Emma bought us ice cream. Now that's magical, not the sand.

The Sand Dilemma

Here's the problem: I'm mad at Lisa, but it was an accident. I want to stay mad for longer, but Aunt Emma looks at me with those eyes that say "forgive your cousin," and it's super hard to stay angry.

Meanwhile, Lisa kept saying "I'm sorry" and making sad faces at me. And to be honest, she looked more like an abandoned puppy than a cousin who had thrown sand in my eyes.

Mom and Aunt Emma sat both of us down and gave us that "family must forgive each other"

talk. So, with a VERY deep sigh, I decided to give Lisa another chance. But I told her that the next time we played in the sand, she would be the tower and I would be the King. That brought a smile to her face, and okay, to mine too.

Aunt Emma made chocolate chip cookies for us at night. How can I stay mad when there are cookies involved? Impossible!

At the end of the day, we played together as if nothing had happened. Although I couldn't help but think that maybe forgiving not only helps the one who receives it but also the one who gives it. Phew, that sounded very grown-up!

Well, tomorrow is another day, and I hope it's full of adventures... but with less sand in my eyes, please!

Sand in the Past

Today, I've been thinking a lot about what happened with the sand and all that. At first, I felt like a pressure cooker about to whistle. But now, I realize that I was angry only because it hurt and scared me, not because Lisa wanted to turn me into a beach snowman.

I've learned something VERY important: talking is like magic. When I told Lisa how I felt, and she explained that it was an accident, the black cloud of my anger flew away. I also found out that forgiving is like throwing away a heavy backpack of rocks. You feel lighter and can run much faster towards the ice cream that Mom takes out of the freezer. Yumm!

Oh, and one more thing: when you don't let accidents turn into a giant monster that eats your fun, you can do more things, like building

the biggest sandcastle in the world with your cousin. Yes, without collapsed towers this time!

Lisa and I made a pact of no more sand in the face. Now we wear diving goggles even on land. Prevention is better than cure!

So, today was a super happy day. Sometimes things don't go as we expect, but that doesn't mean the day has to end badly! With a little dialogue and a lot of forgiveness, we can fix almost anything... except maybe a broken vase. That's a job for super glue.

Until the next adventure!

With fewer tantrums and more castles,

Mason.

Lucas's First Day of School

The Great Adventure Begins

Today is THE day. Yes, that day with capital letters. My first day in elementary school. I'm Lucas, and I'm 6 years old! (almost 7, by the way). I woke up this morning feeling like an astronaut about to go to space. Well, if

astronauts carried backpacks full of notebooks and pencils instead of spacesuits. Mom says I'm going to make a lot of new friends and learn many things. That sounds exciting, but also a little bit scary. What if I can't find the bathroom on time? Or if my teacher is a real-life version of the Witch from "Snow White"? I have a million questions and no answers yet.

My Mom made me the biggest breakfast in the  universe to give me energy. I tried to eat it all, but I think my stomach is nervous too. Then, I put on my new clothes. I chose my dinosaur shirt because, obviously, dinosaurs bring good luck. And today, I need all the luck in the world.

Before leaving, I practiced my smile in the mirror. Dad says a smile is the best introduction. I hope the kids at school think

my smile is nice and not weird. Sometimes, I get a crooked smile when I'm nervous.

When we arrived at school, my heart started racing faster than Flash. Everything is huge here. There are kids everywhere, some running, others laughing. I feel like a tiny fish in a giant ocean. Mom gave me a super tight hug (I almost turned into a Lucas pancake) and told me everything was going to be okay. I want to believe her.

I walked towards the entrance, trying to act natural. It's not easy to act natural when your legs feel like jelly. For a moment, I thought about turning around and running back to mom's car. But then, I remembered my dinosaur on my shirt. Dinosaurs don't run away, right? So, I took a deep breath (three times, to be exact) and walked in.

And here I am! Sitting in my new class, surrounded by new faces. I haven't talked to

anyone yet, but I'm working on gathering the courage. Who knows? Maybe I'll make my first friend today. Or maybe I'll discover that I can count to ten in French. The sky's the limit!

The School Treasure Map

Arriving at school, the next day, I felt that familiar nervous flutter in my stomach. But then I remembered Mom's wise words: "If you get lost, just ask." Sure, that sounds easy for someone who already knows where everything is.

Today was my second expedition into the vast world of elementary school. Yes, I called it an expedition because, honestly, finding my classroom is like searching for treasure without a map. Well, except instead of gold, the treasure is not being late and avoiding the teacher's mean look.

But here comes the fun part. While standing in front of the wall full of papers, trying to understand the puzzle (better known as the class schedule), a kind voice asked, "Can I help you?". There he was, Daniel, with a big smile and his backpack full of superhero stickers (which, by the way, is super cool). It was like a bright light showing me the way to find the class I was looking for.

I showed him my schedule, and it turns out we were going to the same place! Suddenly, the journey didn't feel so lonely. We walked together, and Daniel told me jokes so bad they were good. I don't know how he does that. Making friends didn't seem as hard as yesterday anymore.

We entered the classroom together, and guess what, we didn't get lost once! (Well, maybe we took a little detour, but that counts as a sightseeing tour, right?). The teacher smiled at us when we arrived, and she was

nothing like a Witch, more like the opposite. I wonder if she'll always be so nice or if it's a 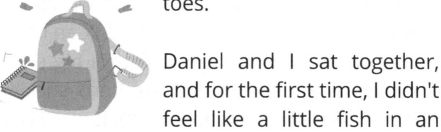 strategy to keep us on our toes.

Daniel and I sat together, and for the first time, I didn't feel like a little fish in an ocean. More like a fish in a... smaller and less intimidating pond. The class flew by with numbers and words, and every time I looked at Daniel, I knew I had found my first treasure on this school treasure map.

So, today I learned that with a little courage (and a friend who knows the way), this expedition called elementary school might not be so scary after all. And who knows, maybe tomorrow I'll discover a new treasure. Or at least learn a new joke.

The Playground Expedition

Today, on my third day of school, let me tell you: what a day at school! I thought finding friends was going to be the hardest part, but it turns out the real challenge was on the playground. Imagine a sea of kids running everywhere, and me trying not to get lost in the crowd!

But I wasn't alone on this adventure; I had Daniel, my new super friend. Together, we decided that if we couldn't play on the swing or the slide because of the crowd, we'd invent our own game. Thus was born "The Playground Expedition". Our goal was simple but exciting: to find the quietest and most secret corner of the playground to make it our own.

After a search worthy of a treasure map, we found a space behind some bushes. It was perfect,

like a little corner of the world just for us. There we decided that every recess would be a new adventure, adding stories and games to our secret base.

The Superpowers of Friendship

Today, as I reflected on our secret base about everything I've experienced since my first day, I realized how much I've grown. Learning to overcome my fears has given me a superpower: the courage to make new friends and face challenges.

Becoming friends with Daniel taught me that asking for help and sharing are acts of bravery. Together, we've created a special place on the playground, but more importantly, we've built a friendship that makes every day at school an exciting adventure.

So, here I am, ready for whatever school brings me. With friends like Daniel by my side,

I know I can face any challenge and turn it into an opportunity to grow and learn. Here's to more adventures and laughter on the playground!

Thank you for being part of this journey. See you in the next adventure!

Lucas.

Stop Being Invisible

Discovering Fear and Invisibility

Hi, I'm James, I'm 6 and a half years old, I live in a loving home with Dad, Mom, and my mischievous cat, Whiskers. I have a superpower that I didn't choose: I can be invisible. Well, not exactly like superheroes, but close. I'm so shy that sometimes I feel like I disappear, especially when I'm at school or in crowded places.

Today, while looking at the school bulletin board, I saw something that made my heart beat faster: a dance contest. I've always loved dancing. In my room, I become a dance star, where no one can see me. But the idea of dancing in front of others... that's more terrifying than a surprise math test.

The problem is big: on one hand, I want to showcase my dance. On the other, my "invisibility" superpower kicks in when I'm most nervous. How am I going to dance on stage if I can't even raise my hand in class to answer a question?

As I walked home, I thought about all the times I wanted to participate in something and ended up hiding. But this time I feel like it could be different. I want to be seen, I want them

to know I exist and that I can do more than just disappear.

My mom says that sometimes we have to face our fears to find out what we're made of. I think it's time to find out what I'm made of. Tomorrow I'm going to sign up for the contest. Well, if my invisibility doesn't decide otherwise.

Can I turn my fear into my dance? I don't know. But one thing's for sure, I want to try. After all, even an invisible superhero has to learn to shine someday.

See you tomorrow. Hopefully with less fear and more courage,

James.

The Value of Facing Fear

Yesterday I decided something really big: I'm going to participate in the school dance contest! Although just thinking about it makes me have butterflies in my stomach. Giant butterflies.

This morning, after breakfast (my mom made my favorite pancakes to cheer me up), I started practicing my dance. I played my favorite song and imagined myself on stage, under the bright lights. At first, I felt a bit clumsy, like a duck on ice skates. But after a while, I started to feel the music and forgot everything else.

However, every time I remembered that I would have to dance in front of real people, not just my stuffed animals, my heart started racing like I was in a marathon. "What if I fall?  What if everyone laughs at me?" I thought. But then I remembered what Mom said: "Every time you feel afraid, take a deep breath and think of something

happy." So I breathed and thought about how it would feel to make the final leap of my dance and hear applause.

Mom saw me practicing and said I was doing an incredible job. That made me feel a little better. She taught me some breathing tricks to calm my nerves and told me something I won't forget: "Fear is just a feeling, James. It can't stop you unless you let it."

In the afternoon, while practicing my dance in the garden, something funny happened. I was trying to do a spin and, oops!, I lost my balance and landed on the grass. For a moment, I wanted to disappear out of embarrassment. But then, from the window, I heard Mom laughing and applauding. That made me laugh too. If I can laugh at my mistakes, maybe the stage won't be so scary after all.

So here I am, ending my day feeling a little braver. Tomorrow I'm going to keep

practicing, and who knows, maybe I'll discover that I have more courage than I thought,

James.

Overcoming on Stage

Today was the day of the big dance contest and, wow, what a roller coaster of emotions. The morning started with a knot in my stomach so big I thought I had swallowed a basketball. Seriously, even breakfast seemed like an impossible mountain to climb. "What if I just don't go?" I thought for a moment. But then, I remembered all the times Mom told me that facing my fears is the only way to overcome them.

Getting to the contest venue was like walking towards a giant castle. My legs were shaking so much I almost did a new dance called "the shakies." Waiting behind the curtain, watching other kids perform their acts, my heart was pounding like a giant drum.

"It's now or never," I told myself. And just before it was my turn, I closed my eyes, took three deep breaths (just like Mom taught me), and thought of my lucky Dinosaur. "Dinosaurs aren't afraid," I told myself.

Then, I heard my name. "James, it's your turn!"

I opened my eyes, and with my "brave face" on (the same one I practiced with Mom), I walked onto the stage. The music started, and for a second, all my fear evaporated. It was just me, the music, and my dance.

I don't know how, but as I danced, I felt like I was flying. Every step, every spin, felt perfect. And when I finished, with a final leap I practiced a thousand times, the room filled with applause. Applause for me! For a moment, I forgot how to breathe. Were they applauding... for me?

After the performance, several people came to tell me how much they liked my dance. Even Liam, a boy I I met in the hallway, said it was "super cool." I never imagined I could feel this happy and proud of myself.

So here I am, ending the day feeling like a true superstar. I learned that fear is just a ghost that shrinks when you dare to confront it. And that sometimes, all you need to fly is to take the first step... or in my case, the first dance. Now I know that, even though fear may be big, my courage is even bigger.

James's Transformation

After an incredible day, here I am, sitting in my room, thinking about everything that has happened.

Today, as I looked at myself in the mirror, I noticed something different. No, I didn't grow

4 inches overnight (although that would have been awesome), but I did see a James that I didn't know before. A James who dares to dance on stage in front of lots and lots of people.

I thought about all the fears I had before the contest: "What if I mess up? What if everyone laughs? What if...?" But then, I remembered that magical moment on stage, where everything disappeared except the music and me. And I realized something super important: the "what ifs...?"s aren't as terrible as they seem.

I learned that believing in myself is like having a superpower. Yes, it sounds like something a fairytale character would say, but it's true. When you believe you can do something, suddenly the world is filled with possibilities.

Another super important thing I learned is that facing my fears is the only way to overcome them. Yes, it's a bit like facing a giant

monster (or a bunch of curious stares), but once you do it, you realize that the monster wasn't as big as you thought.

And here comes the coolest part: being visible has its rewards. After the contest, people who had never talked to me came to say nice things about my dance. I even made some new friends, and that's something the invisible James would never have accomplished!

I'm excited for what's to come. With every new challenge, I know I can grow a little more. And although I know there will be more fears in the future, I also know that I have what it takes to face them.

See you in the next adventure! I'm ready for whatever comes, with a little bit of nerves, of course, but with a lot more courage.

.

The Giant Slide

The Great Adventure Begins

Hello, I'm Henry, a 6-year-old with an adventurous spirit who absolutely loves amusement parks. I want to share with you the beginning of an incredible story!

The amusement park has finally arrived in town, and I am jumping with excitement. Adventures are my thing, and what's more

adventurous than a park filled with rides and attractions? But there's one in particular that has me counting stars before sleep: the Giant Yellow Slide. It's a slide so big it seems to touch the sky. Although I adore facing these kinds of challenges, this one gives me a special tingle in my stomach.

Imagine this: me, Henry, the most adventurous of all, launching myself down that gigantic yellow curve, screaming at the top of my lungs with my arms raised high. It would be the talk of recess for weeks. Of course, as long as I don't close my eyes all the way down. My best friend, Liam, says I'm going to fly like a superhero. I just hope my cape doesn't get tangled.

Although I'm a little nervous (just a little, I promise), I'm determined. Tomorrow, I'm going to face the Giant Yellow Slide and I'm going to win. Well, at least I'm not going to let it beat me.

So, keep your fingers crossed for me. Tomorrow is the day I become a legend of the amusement park!

With a pinch of nerves and tons of excitement.

A Sea of Adventures and the Giant Yellow Slide

Today dawned a radiant day and it was a day full of adventures in the amusement park. First, I went to the bumper cars, where I felt like a race car driver dodging everyone else. I even won three times in a row! Then, I tried the swinging pirate ship. At first, it was fun to feel how it went up and down, but after the fifth time, my stomach started to think it was in a blender and the breakfast I had in the morning wanted to make its appearance.

Although I had a lot of fun, I couldn't stop looking towards the Giant Yellow Slide. Every time I saw someone slide down it, a part of me wanted to join in and scream with excitement, but another part wanted to run in the opposite direction. It's like having an angel on one shoulder and a little devil on the other, and I can't decide which one to listen to.

Mom says it's okay to be afraid, that it's normal, but also that sometimes, to have fun, we have to face those fears. Although today I didn't become the legend, tomorrow we will go back to the park again and I think it might be the day I finally line up for the Giant Yellow Slide. Wish for the angel to win!

Facing the Giant

Today I finally gathered all my courage to face the Giant Yellow Slide.

While in line, my legs were shaking like jello on a plate. Every step forward made me want to take two steps back. But then, Mom gave me that little push of bravery I needed.

"Think of this as one of your superhero adventures," mom said. "Even superheroes feel fear, but they overcome it to save the day." That made me smile. Who would have thought that I, Henry, could be a superhero for a day?

When my turn came, I closed my eyes, took three deep breaths as my Mom taught me, and launched myself. For a second, all I could feel was the wind on my face and my heart beating hard. But then, I opened my eyes and... Wow! It was the most exciting ride of my life. In the end, I was so happy I wanted to do it again, so I don't remember how many

more times that I went down it!

Thanks to my Mom's advice and my own bravery, today I learned that it's okay to be afraid, but not to let that fear stop you. Thank you, Mom, for helping me see that. The Giant Yellow Slide is nothing compared to the bravery of a boy with an imaginary cape!

Looking Back with Bravery

Today, as I sit here thinking about my adventure with the Giant Yellow Slide, I realize how much I've grown. Facing my fear was not only exciting but also taught me a great lesson about bravery and self-confidence. With my mom's support, I discovered that I can do anything, even if it seems impossible at first.

I've realized that fears are just shadows that become smaller when you decide to face them. And although I know I will encounter many more fears along the way, I now have the bravery to face them one by one.

This journey has taught me that family support is like an invisible superhero cape that always accompanies me. I want to remember this moment every time I face a new challenge.

So, thank you for being here to listen (or rather, read) my adventures. Until the next adventure!

Hidden Talent

A Great Challenge on the Horizon

Hello! My name is Jacob, I'm 6 years old, and I live in a small town where almost everyone knows each other. My life is pretty normal: I go to school, play with my friends, and spend time with my family. But there's something I love more than anything else: singing and acting. I feel like a star every time I get to step

on a stage or even when I put on small shows in my living room for my parents.

Today at school, our teacher gave us exciting news: we're going to put on a play, and it's not just any play, it's "Romeo and Juliet"! And here's the best part of it all: I was chosen to be Romeo! Imagine, my dream of acting and singing in front of everyone is about to come true.

But not everything is as perfect as it sounds. There's a pretty big "but" in this story, and that "but" has a name: Abby. Yes, you read that right. Abby, the shyest and quietest girl in the whole school, will be my Juliet.

The moment the teacher announced her name, I could swear the world stopped for a second. We all stood there with our mouths open,

including her, who seemed to want the earth to swallow her up.

When I got home, I couldn't help but tell my parents everything. My mom, always so positive, told me that maybe this would be a good opportunity for Abby and that I should give her a chance. But, you know? I'm really worried. What if Abby can't overcome her shyness? What if our play doesn't go well because of this? I want it to be perfect, every single day.

I've decided I'm going to do something about it. I can't just sit around waiting for things to fix themselves. Tomorrow, I'm going to talk to Abby before rehearsals. Maybe, between the two of us, we can find a way to make her feel more comfortable on stage.

Action plan: Turn Abby into the best Juliet our little town has ever seen. It's time to act, in every sense of the word!

With determination,
Jacob, the Romeo with a mission.

A Musical Surprise

Today was one of those days that made you see everything differently. After class, I went to Abby's house to practice our parts of the play. I was super nervous. Not just about the rehearsal, but about how we were going to work together.

Abby lives in a house that looks like it's from a storybook, with a garden full of flowers and a stone path leading to the door. Her mom greeted me with a huge smile and led me to her room. And here's the incredible part!

When I opened the door, Abby was playing the piano! But not just anything... she was playing one of the songs from our play, and it sounded...

magical. I never would have imagined that the shy girl in class had a talent like that. It was like discovering that my classmate was a musical superhero.

I couldn't help it; I stood there, wide-eyed, listening to her play until she finished. And when she did, I applauded her as if I were at the most impressive concert of my life. Abby blushed a lot and told me she felt embarrassed to play in front of others. Embarrassed! With that talent, she should be giving concerts.

So, right then and there, my mission changed. It was no longer just about making our play a success. Now it was also about helping Abby share her incredible talent with everyone. The world needs to hear her!

We practiced together, and believe me, when Abby forgets about her fear, it's like she transforms. In fact, she even taught me some tricks with her voice. Turns out, she's not only

a piano genius, she also knows a lot about singing. Who would have thought!

At the end of the day, I went home with a mix of excitement and admiration. Abby is not only going to surprise everyone in the play, I think we're going to make a spectacular team. And to think that all this time she was there, hidden behind her shyness.

So never underestimate anyone. Everyone has something special to show.

With enthusiasm,
Jacob, the talent detective turned singer.

The Day of the Big Surprise

Today was the big day of the play, and I have so much to tell you. I was so excited and nervous that I could hardly eat breakfast. But the most important thing today wasn't my nervousness, but what happened with Abby.

We arrived early at school, and the gym was already transformed into a big theater. Behind the stage, we were all a little nervous, but no one was more than Abby. I saw her there, as quiet as always, and I thought, "Today, everyone is going to see how amazing she is."

And then, the play began. Everything was going well, and the most awaited moment arrived: the first song. I took a breath, looked at Abby, and something magical happened. When the music started, Abby transformed. She wasn't the shy girl we all knew. She was... a rockstar Juliet! She sang with such a loud and clear voice that for a second, everyone was silent, as if they couldn't believe what they were hearing.

And then, applause! Lots and lots of applause. Our classmates, the teachers, the parents, everyone was on their feet, applauding like crazy. It was the most amazing moment of my life.

After the play, everyone wanted to talk to Abby, congratulate her, and ask her how long she has known how to sing like that. I saw the surprise on their faces, just like the surprise I had the first day I heard her. And Abby, well, she just smiled, a little overwhelmed, but happy.

Now, I'm more excited than ever for what's to come. Because after today, I know there are stories, talents, and surprises waiting for us, we just have to be ready to discover them.

With a heart full of music and surprises, Jacob, the talent detective and Abby's number one fan.

A Bunch of New Things

Today, I'm thinking about everything that has happened these last few days. It was a huge adventure, full of music, nerves, and a big

surprise named Abby. After yesterday's play, I've been reflecting a lot on everything I learned.

We should never, ever judge people just by how they look or what we think we know about them. Abby taught me that. And today's play... well, it showed everyone that everyone has something special and something shining, inside. We just need the opportunity to let it out.

Then there's the issue of fear. I was afraid of how the play would turn out, and Abby was afraid of showing herself as she is. But together, we learned that facing those fears makes us stronger. It's like when you swing to the highest point and feel like you're going to fly; it's a little scary, but also super exciting.

I also learned about empathy and courage. Helping Abby feel safe and seeing how everyone changed their opinion about her was

something very special. It reminded me that everyone carries something cool inside, it's just that sometimes we need a little help to show it. It's like when you team up at recess and realize that together, everyone has more fun.

So, here I go, ready for whatever comes, with my ears open to listen to more stories and my heart ready to meet more friends like Abby. Because now I know that every day can be an adventure, and I'm excited to discover what surprises await me.

With a little song in my heart and a bunch of new ideas in my head,

Jacob.

96300589R00049